T 63627

Library of Congress Cataloging in Publication Data

Burgess, Thornton W.   1874–1965

BOBBY COON & REDDY FOX PLAY TRICKS

Summary: Returning home from a night of mischief in the woods,
Bobby Coon and Reddy Fox discover the tables have been turned.

1. Fantasy — Fiction   I. McQueen, Lucinda, ill.

II. Title

Library of Congress Catalog Card Number 90-071313
Series 1 Number 1

ISBN 0-938715-04-6
Printed in Singapore
Published January 1991
First Printing

This book was typeset in Goudy Old Style and composed by
Alternative Ink, Albany, New York.

Editor: Edward Dowling
Designer: Larry Weir
Art Director: John Gunther

To My Brother

Bill

– LM

Bobby Coon
&
Reddy Fox
PLAY TRICKS

BY THORNTON W. BURGESS

ILLUSTRATED BY LUCINDA MCQUEEN

It was night. All the little stars were looking down and twinkling and twinkling. Mother Moon was doing her best to make the Green Meadows as light as Mr. Sun did in the daytime. All the little birds except Hooty the Owl and Boomer the Night Hawk and noisy Mr. Whippoorwill were fast asleep in their little nests. Old Mother West Wind's Merry Little Breezes had all gone to sleep, too. It was oh so still!

Indeed it was so very still that Bobby Coon, coming down the
Lone Little Path through the wood, began to talk to himself.

"I don't see what people want to play all day and sleep all night
for," said Bobby Coon. "Night's the best time to be about. Now
Reddy Fox—"

"Be careful what you say about Reddy Fox," said a voice right behind Bobby Coon.

Bobby Coon turned around very quickly indeed, for he had thought he was all alone. There was Reddy Fox himself, trotting down the Lone Little Path through the wood.

"I thought you were home and fast asleep, Reddy Fox," said Bobby Coon.

"You were mistaken," said Reddy Fox, "for you see I'm out to take a walk in the moonlight."

So Bobby Coon and Reddy Fox walked together down the Lone Little Path through the wood to Green Meadows.

They met Jimmy Skunk, who had dreamed that there were a lot of beetles up on the hill, and was going to climb the Crooked Little Path to see.

"Hello, Jimmy Skunk!" said Bobby Coon and Reddy Fox. "Come down to the Green Meadows with us."

Jimmy Skunk said he would, so they all went down on the Green Meadows together, Bobby Coon first, Reddy Fox next, and Jimmy Skunk last of all, for Jimmy Skunk never hurries.

Pretty soon they came to the house of Johnny Chuck.

"Listen," said Bobby Coon, "Johnny Chuck is fast asleep."

They all listened, and they could hear Johnny Chuck snoring away down in his snug little bed.

"Let's give Johnny Chuck a surprise," said Reddy Fox.

"What shall it be?" asked Bobby Coon.

"I know," said Reddy Fox. "Let's roll that big stone right over Johnny Chuck's doorway. Then he will have to dig his way out in the morning."

So Bobby Coon and Reddy Fox pulled and tugged and tugged and pulled at the big stone till they had rolled it over Johnny Chuck's doorway. Jimmy Skunk pretended not to see what they were doing.

"Now let's go down to the Laughing Brook and wake up old Grandfather Frog and hear him say 'Chug-arum,' " said Bobby Coon.

"Come on!" cried Reddy Fox. "I'll get there first!"

Away raced Reddy Fox down the Lone Little Path and after him ran Bobby Coon, going to wake old Grandfather Frog from a nice comfortable sleep on his green lily pad.

But Jimmy Skunk didn't go. He watched Reddy Fox and Bobby
Coon until they were nearly to the Laughing Brook. Then he began
to dig at one side of the big stone which filled the doorway of Johnny
Chuck's house. My, how he made the dirt fly!

Pretty soon he had made a hole big enough to call through to
Johnny Chuck, who was snoring away, fast asleep in his snug little
bed below.

"Johnny Chuck, Chuck, Chuck! Johnny Woodchuck!" called
Jimmy Skunk. But Johnny Chuck just snored.

"Johnny Chuck, Chuck, Chuck! Johnny Woodchuck!" called
Jimmy Skunk once more. But Johnny Chuck just snored.

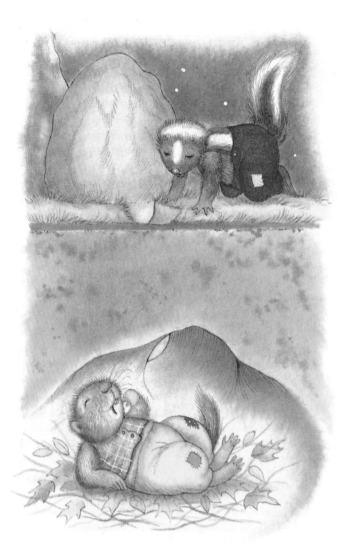

Then Jimmy Skunk called again, this time louder than before.

"Who is it?" asked a very sleepy voice.

"It's Jimmy Skunk. Put your coat on and come up here!" called Jimmy Skunk.

"Go away, Jimmy Skunk. I want to sleep!" said Johnny Chuck.

"I've got a surprise for you, Johnny Chuck. You'd better come!" called Jimmy Skunk through the little hole he had made.

When Johnny Chuck heard that Jimmy Skunk had a surprise for him he wanted to know right away what it could be, so though he was very, very sleepy, he put on his coat and started up to his door to see what the surprise was that Jimmy Skunk had.

And there he found the big stone Reddy Fox and Bobby Coon
had put there, and of course he was very much surprised indeed. He
thought Jimmy Skunk had played a mean trick, and for a few minutes
he was very mad. But Jimmy Skunk soon told him who had filled up
his doorway with the big stone.

"Now you push from that side, Johnny Chuck, and I'll pull from this side, and we'll soon have this big stone out of your doorway," said Jimmy Skunk.

So Johnny Chuck pushed and Jimmy Skunk pulled, and sure enough, they soon had the big stone out of Johnny Chuck's doorway.

"Now," said Jimmy Skunk, "we'll roll this big stone down the Lone Little Path to Reddy Fox's house and we'll give Reddy Fox a surprise."

So Johnny Chuck and
Jimmy Skunk tugged and pulled
and rolled the big stone down to
the house of Reddy Fox, and sure
enough, it filled his doorway.

"Good night, Jimmy Skunk," said
Johnny Chuck, and trotted down the
Lone Little Path toward home,
chuckling to himself all the way.

Jimmy Skunk walked slowly up the Lone Little Path to the wood for Jimmy Skunk never hurries.

Pretty soon he came to the big hollow tree where Bobby Coon lives, and there he met Hooty the Owl.

"Hello, Jimmy Skunk, where have you been?" asked Hooty the Owl.

"Just for a walk," said Jimmy Skunk. "Who lives in this big hollow tree?"

Now of course, Jimmy Skunk knew all the time, but he pretended he didn't.

"Oh, this is Bobby Coon's house," said Hooty the Owl.

"Let's give Bobby Coon a surprise," said Jimmy Skunk.

"How?" asked Hooty the Owl.

"We'll fill his house full of sticks and leaves," said Jimmy Skunk.

Hooty the Owl thought that would be a good joke, so while Jimmy Skunk gathered all the old sticks and leaves he could find, Hooty the Owl stuffed them into the old hollow tree, which was Bobby Coon's house, until he couldn't get in another one.

"Good night," said Jimmy Skunk, as he began to climb the Crooked Little Path up the hill to his own snug little home.

"Good night," said Hooty the Owl, as he flew like a big soft shadow over to the Great Pine.

By and by, when old Mother Moon was just going to bed and all the little stars were too sleepy to twinkle any longer, Reddy Fox and Bobby Coon, very tired and very wet from playing in the Laughing Brook, came up the Lone Little Path, ready to tumble into their snug little beds. They were chuckling over the trick they had played on Johnny Chuck, and the way they had waked up old Grandfather Frog, and all the other mischief they had done.

What do you suppose they said when they reached their homes and found that someone else had been playing jokes, too?

I'm sure I don't know, but round, red Mr. Sun was laughing very hard as he peeped over the hill at Reddy Fox and Bobby Coon, and he won't tell why.